NOV 04 2005

HOLDEN PUBLIC LIBRARY

3 2814 0003 1491 0

W9-ASN-203

WITHDRAWN FROM LIBRARY

NOV 04 2005

HOLDEN PUBLIC LIBRARY

W9-ASN-203

What in the World?

Bartolomeo Cristofori's 1720 piano is the oldest in the world, but it was restored in 1938 and includes parts that were not original. It remains in playable condition.

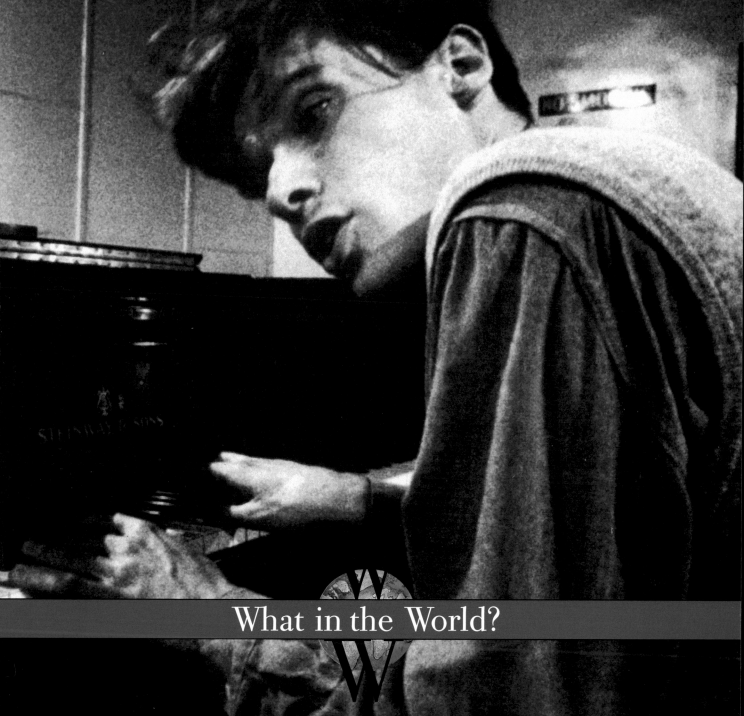

What in the World?

Creative Education

Introduction

He wanted quiet. So Bartolomeo Cristofori sought an escape from the clatter of the crowded studio where a Florentine prince had put him to work. He carried home the tools of his trade and proceeded in solitude, building a new sort of musical instrument— one that could give him quiet of a different kind, a sound both subtle and expressive in pitch. He created a machine, complex in its thousands of parts, but simple in its mission. He made the piano, a creation that could match the human voice's ability to range from soft to loud and reflect the full emotion of the musician.

Spinets, virginals, and harpsichords belong to the same family. All are keyboard instruments with strings sounded by a plucking device. The harpsichord, however, is much larger and louder than its musical cousins.

A fancifully decorated virginal dating from 1661.

Hammers and strings make up the beautifully complex inner workings of the piano.

Jan Vermeer's Girl with a Pearl Earring, *created in 1665.*

Rembrandt's final autobiographical painting, Self Portrait Aged 63.

Dutch painter Jan Vermeer rose to prominence in the late 1600s and was known for the poetic quality of his images and the delicacy with which he rendered effects of light and color. Only 36 paintings attributed to Vermeer exist today.

Rembrandt van Rijn was a master at using light in his works. He became the leading portrait painter in Holland in the late 17th century and received many commissions for both portraits and paintings of religious subjects.

Bartolomeo Cristofori arrived in the Italian city of Florence in 1688, just as Europe moved into an era that would become known as the Age of Enlightenment. Music and art enjoyed high status in the Medici palace, where Bartolomeo worked as an instrument maker. It was a peaceful corner in an expanding world that was increasingly full of change and struggle.

People of the time believed that mankind was entering its maturity, leaving behind an era of darkness and ignorance. They questioned the notion that all of life's truths—from physics to philosophy—had been described by the ancient Greeks and Romans, or in the Bible. Such curious individuals as English scientist Isaac Newton had shown that careful thought and study could unlock many of the world's greatest mysteries.

Englishman Isaac Newton published the book *Principia* in 1686, detailing his theories of motion and gravity. The work, sparked 20 years earlier by his observance of a falling apple, created the foundation of the study of physics.

Isaac Newton developed many mathematical tools and initiated theories that dominated science for centuries.

Immanuel Kant's thoughts on human knowledge had a profound impact on many philosophical movements.

Leading thinkers of the late 1600s put great stock in human reason, promoting the observation of nature and a devotion to education. Although they maintained their belief in a higher power, many of the top minds of the time criticized organized religion, especially the Catholic Church, for limiting individual liberty and intellectual discovery. German philosopher Immanuel Kant summed up the Age of Enlightenment when he wrote, "Dare to know! Have the courage to use your intelligence!"

In 1680, Pueblo tribes drove away Spanish missionaries who were trying to convert the Native Americans to Christianity and destroyed Spanish churches built in the region that is now New Mexico.

Many Jesuit missionaries were sent to try to convert Native Americans to Christianity in the 17th century.

This 1531 woodcut suggests the uneasy balance of power in Europe in the 16th and 17th centuries.

Although Europe's intellectuals considered themselves enlightened, its rulers still relied heavily on brute force. Widespread exploration in the 1500s and 1600s had fueled the formation of colonies around the world, and distant lands fell under the rule of France, Spain, England, Portugal, and other countries. The powers of Europe rushed to claim new territory, leading to conflicts with native peoples and tensions between the colonial powers themselves.

Paper money first came into use in Europe in the mid-1600s, although Europeans had known about Chinese paper money for hundreds of years. Banks issued their own paper notes, which could be exchanged for gold or silver coins.

Native Americans fought to save their lands in South Carolina, but in 1715, they were defeated by British settlers. The Yamassees (or Savannahs) and other tribes were driven south into Florida, then Spanish territory.

France, Spain, and England all claimed shares of North America, disregarding the rights of the millions of American Indians who had long lived on the land. French explorer René Robert Cavelier, Sieur de La Salle declared the entire Mississippi Valley the property of his country in 1682, and the French soon built New Orleans where the river flowed into the Gulf of Mexico. Spain controlled Florida and other territories in the South and West, and British colonies grew on the Atlantic coast; 11 of the original 13 British colonies were established by 1700. The white population of the colonies flourished as much of their economic strength was built on the backs of African slaves.

René Robert Cavelier, Sieur de La Salle claimed "Louisiana" for his homeland and King Louis XIV on April 9, 1682.

The Great Northern War pitted Sweden against neighboring forces led by Russia's Peter the Great. Fighting over territory around the Baltic Sea began in 1700 and lasted until the Swedes surrendered in 1721.

The Battle of Poltava in 1709 was a victory for Russia's Peter the Great in the Great Northern War.

War broke out after Spanish king Charles II died and left no heir. The War of Spanish Succession began in 1701 and lasted 12 years, as neighboring nations battled over Spain's territory.

This work by French artist Puvis de Chavannes depicts a scene from the War of Spanish Succession.

This painting, created in 1562 by Flemish artist Theodor de Bry, depicts natives attacking a colonial village in Brazil.

South America, too, was dominated by European powers. Spain had a vast presence there, and the Portuguese controlled Brazil, having established the city of Rio de Janeiro in the late 1500s. In the 1700s, Brazil would become the center of the huge South American coffee bean industry. Coffee trees were not native to the area but were planted by Europeans eager to support the growing fashion of coffee drinking back home.

Tensions between native Brazilians and Portuguese settlers erupted around the merchant city of Recife in 1710. The Portuguese prevailed and asserted their control as an imperial power.

This woodcut (opposite) shows South American natives picking ripe coffee beans for export to Europe.

Some Africans sold their brethren as slaves (above) in the late 1600s.

The first streetlights were introduced in London during the mid-1680s. They were oil-burning lamps built with reflectors to illuminate the area below.

Africa had long been ruled by a mix of native empires and kingdoms, each with its own language and customs. But by the late 1600s, several European nations had established trading posts in Africa. The demand for slaves in North America resulted in millions of Africans being ripped from their home-lands and shipped across the Atlantic for sale to colonists. Even Africans themselves were corrupted by the slave trade. The Asante empire, established in the 1680s on the West African coast, grew wealthy by selling gold and slaves captured from other tribes.

A lamplighter igniting a streetlight in London (left)

Early piano-like instruments influenced art, as in Italian painter Orazio Gentileschi's Saint Cecilia Playing the Spinet with Angel.

Post roads allowed American colonists to exchange mail and grew in importance as America expanded westward.

Regular mounted mail delivery began in the American colonies during the 1670s, and the first post road established ran between New York and Boston. Soon other post roads created links between the colonies.

As these turbulent events unfolded, Bartolomeo Cristofori lived a quiet, anonymous life in Florence. He was not famous, and never would be. He was an expert on the harpsichord, a keyboard instrument with strings set inside a wing-shaped frame. Bartolomeo knew the instrument and its shortcomings well and used his knowledge to begin work on a new machine—one that would eventually change music around the world forever.

The lyre piano was one of four upright piano styles (along with "pyramid," "bookcase," and "giraffe") produced in the early 1800s.

A Musical Pioneer

It seems improbable that an object as familiar and almost constantly present in the lives of people today as the piano could have come from the hands of an inventor whose life remains obscure and largely forgotten. But that is the case with Bartolomeo Cristofori and his creation, which he called the *gravicembalo col piano e forte,* or "harpsichord with soft and loud." The name was soon shortened to pianoforte, or piano.

Cristofori's skill as an instrument maker went beyond keyboard instruments such as the harpsichord and included stringed instruments such as double basses and violoncellos.

Bartolomeo's early life is mostly lost to history. He was born in 1655 in the city of Padua, Italy. Almost nothing is known of his childhood and education, which led him to a career as an instrument maker who specialized in harpsichords, one of the piano's nearest musical ancestors. One thing is clear, however: Bartolomeo must have built an impressive reputation, because in 1688, he was recruited to work in the prestigious court of Prince Ferdinando de Medici in Florence, Italy.

The 18th-century Italian accordo *took a prominent place among stringed instruments of the time.*

Marrying a body of spruce and maple

to strings of horsehair—the art of violinmaking—

was a delicate endeavor.

The piano has outlasted other instruments and gained popularity largely because of its usefulness as a musical accompaniment.

In Bartolomeo's time, Florence thrived as a cultural hotbed as prominent as Paris or any other leading city of Europe. Prince Ferdinando—with funds provided by his father, Duke Cosimo—had built a sprawling collection of art and musical instruments.

But he was more than a collector. He surrounded himself with painters, sculptors, and craftspeople of all kinds, who together formed a kind of factory for world-class art.

As many as 100 artisans practiced their trades in the Medici court, many of them at work simultaneously and in close quarters. The open floor plan of their shared workspace—and the din created by a busy mix of painters, clockmakers, printers, and so on—became a source of irritation for Bartolomeo. He grew tired of the palace's constant distractions and noise and eventually moved his tools and supplies to his nearby residence, which became his personal workshop.

Duke Cosimo de Medici

While Cristofori was at work in Florence, the Salem witch trials raged in colonial America. In 1692, 150 people were tried for witchcraft. Nineteen were convicted and hanged; others were jailed.

Heavy drinking was common in American colonies, where more than 2.1 million gallons (7.9 million l) of rum were imported in 1728 alone. It came from the Caribbean, along with molasses to supply colonial rum-makers.

The Salem witch trials in colonial America became a lesson in the evils of sensationalism and inspired much literature and art.

Cristofori's first pianos played two strings per note, but in 1722, he developed a hand stop, or lever, that let the player direct the hammer to just one string, softening the sound much like today's players do with a foot pedal.

The legs and base of Cristofori's 1726 piano were destroyed during World War II, but the instrument survived. It remains playable and has been used for recordings that demonstrate the sound of the earliest pianos.

While Europe furthered the development of organ-like instruments in the late 1600s, China perfected porcelain pottery.

Bartolomeo was assigned the significant task of caring for the prince's keyboard instruments, including their constant upkeep and tuning, and their safe transport. As the prince owned 35 such instruments, this was no small job. Still, Bartolomeo found time to experiment, modifying and improving his instruments.

The lineage of keyboard instruments already was centuries old, dating to a time before the year 300 when the first organs were made. The keyboard allowed the organ player to send air through a range of pipes, enabling a single musician to, in effect, blow into many pipes at once. It wasn't long before the keyboard, which put so much musical potential at one person's fingertips, was adapted to make other kinds of sounds—especially those more subtle than an organ's echoing blasts and toots. Eventually, a keyboard was affixed to a stringed instrument.

In this painting by Italian artist Giuseppe Zocchi, many early instruments are in play.

A crude, single-reeded instrument called the chalumeau *was the predecessor to more complex and versatile clarinets.*

The clarinet was invented around the same time as the piano. German instrument maker Johann Christopher Denner made the first clarinet sometime in the 1690s, although similar instruments had existed for some time.

Like a guitar or violin, a piano makes music from the vibration of strings, which are pulled at high tension across a sound board, a thin piece of wood whose vibrations strengthen the sound of the instrument. Stringed instruments have a history that stretches back to humble beginnings in Africa and Southeast Asia about 5,000 years ago. These early instruments had one or more strings that were pulled tight between two bridges, or raised pieces, and pulled or struck to produce sound. Stringed instruments evolved in many ways over the centuries, taking a variety of shapes, sizes, and names.

Stringed instruments have grown dramatically in form and popularity since their inception nearly 5,000 years ago.

By Bartolomeo's time, two popular keyboard instruments had emerged, and strings produced the sounds in both. The harpsichord and the clavichord both appeared in the early 1400s but differed in the way the strings were made to vibrate. When the player pressed keys on a harpsichord, a mechanism inside plucked the strings. The strings of a clavichord, on the other hand, were struck by a series of mallets.

The medieval European zither was a box with 30 to 45 strings stretched from end to end. Similar stringed instruments—plucked like a guitar resting on its side—existed under many names worldwide.

A woman playing a zither, which has also gone by the names of dulcimer, guitar-zither, autoharp, and psaltery.

This illustration depicts Wolfgang Amadeus Mozart composing on the clavichord; his personal clavichord still exists in Austria.

Although popular, the harpsichord and clavichord were flawed instruments. The harpsichord's weakness was a shortage of expressiveness; whether the key was pressed gently or banged with force, the sound produced was the same. The clavichord did not have that problem. A gently pressed key produced a soft note, while volume increased when more force was applied. The trouble was that the clavichord was too quiet in general. It was fine in homes, where it might accompany a solo singer, but it could not fill a large room or team with other instruments supporting a choir.

The appearance of the 17th-century harpsichord was graceful. It was larger than a clavichord and was often built in an ornate wooden case with a long, wing-shaped frame to house the strings, similar to today's grand pianos.

The earliest harpsichord, called a "clavicembalum," was recorded to exist in 1397, while the first evidence of the clavichord's existence dates from 1404.

The harpsichord had the same outward appearance as the piano but lacked the concert hall-grade power that the piano would supply.

Cristofori's piano had no foot pedals. They were added by later makers to manipulate the sound—lifting dampers to sustain a sound or allowing the piano to be played more quietly.

Bartolomeo's bit of genius was to solve both of these problems. In doing so, he answered a need of composers, or writers of music, who were testing the limits of keyboard instruments and bumping up against the shortcomings of existing options. He built something revolutionary inside a plain-looking version of a harpsichord frame. Although his instrument looked familiar, its musical potential, when finally tapped, would be unlike anything the world had ever seen.

Flemish painter Jan Sanders van Hemessen's 1550 painting A Woman at the Clavichord.

Cristofori's musical invention was masterfully played two centuries later by American pianist Arthur Rubinstein.

Bartolomeo's Machine

The rise of the piano followed an arc quite different from that of most successful inventions. It was not a heralded new device that grabbed attention and seemed immediately useful. Bartolomeo had created a complicated device that was superior yet similar to popular instruments of the age. The piano had to be refined and perfected before it would be recognized as the pinnacle in the evolution of keyboard instruments and not just a curious offshoot along the way.

Italians were interested in the power of the human voice and warmth of bowed instruments at the time Cristofori created the first piano, which helps explain why the new instrument was at first neglected.

Pianos are unlike instruments whose roots can be traced back to crude implements of ancient times, when a person could blow through a hollow animal horn or an empty shell to produce simple music. Unlike many modern instruments, such as horns, that still bear a direct connection to their beginnings, keyboard instruments have always been machines whose origins are in the imagination and craftiness of human beings.

The violin became a very popular instrument largely due to its ability to express human-like sound.

Bartolomeo's unique genius lay in creating a new device to control the way the strings vibrated. Like a clavichord, Bartolomeo's instrument featured a row of hammers that struck a set of strings from below. From there, however, the new instrument left behind old ways. Bartolomeo's piano was completely responsive to the touch of the player; a soft touch meant a quiet note, and a hard touch meant a loud note. Bartolomeo also devised a mechanism that sent each hammer up to hit the string and instantly back down, regardless of whether the player released the key. This allowed players to rapidly repeat notes. Bartolomeo's new device also dampened the vibration of the string soon after it was struck, creating a clean, crisp note rather than a racket that reverberated on and on.

Daniel Fahrenheit, a German scientist, created a new scale for measuring temperature and devised a mercury-filled thermometer in 1714.

Fashionable men and women alike wore wigs and tall heels in colonial America around 1710. Men also wore long, stiff coats with sleeve cuffs that stretched from elbow to wrist.

This portrait of American president John Adams, created in 1770, illustrates the meticulously detailed dress code of the time.

Frenchman Paul Cézanne's painting Young Woman at the Piano *shows the piano in a home setting, something Cristofori never witnessed.*

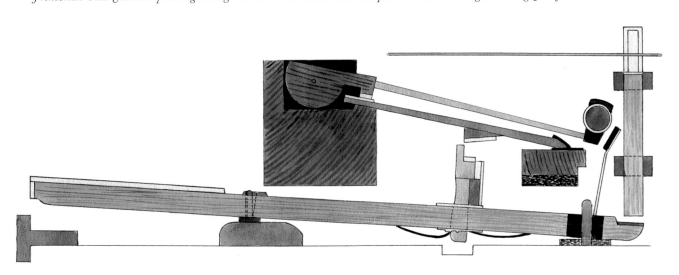

With the adaptation of the hammer dulcimer, the piano's range of expression became greater than that of any other keyboard instrument.

The first written record of Bartolomeo's breakthrough appeared in *The Medici Inventory of Diverse Musical Instruments*, which listed "a large keyboard instrument that produces loud and soft." That publication was dated 1700, the same year the piano is believed to have been invented. Bartolomeo's clever machine, which allowed a range of sounds from subtle to bombastic, brought him little fame during his lifetime. Although Prince Ferdinando and others knowledgeable about music were impressed, the instrument was not immediately embraced in Italy, where opera dominated the musical scene.

A 1711 article in an Italian journal played a vital role in preventing the piano from fading into history. The writer, a journalist from Rome named Scipione Maffei, had visited Bartolomeo two years earlier. This is believed to be the reason why, until recently, many history books placed the invention of the piano in 1709. Maffei's article described Bartolomeo's invention and included a diagram of how it worked.

Describing Cristofori's invention in 1711, Roman journalist Scipione Maffei wrote, "[The] greatest opposition that this new instrument has suffered consists in the fact that people in general do not know how to play it...."

The Mogul empire in India fell apart after the 1707 death of Emperor Aurangzeb, starting years of violence between groups seeking control, including the French, English, and regional rulers from India and neighboring nations.

As an archaeologist, scholar, playwright, and journalist, Scipione Maffei was a man of many talents.

After Cristofori died, Italy lost interest in the piano for a time. By the late 1700s, pianos made in Vienna and elsewhere had gained popularity, but Italy did not begin manufacturing its own pianos again until the 1840s.

In the mid-1720s, Gottfried Silbermann read a German translation of Scipione Maffei's article about the Cristofori piano and immediately began building two instruments he called "harpsichords with hammers."

Bartolomeo would not live to see his instrument's success. When he died in 1731, his life was much as it had been before he built the first piano. Harpsichords remained his specialty, although he had continued to improve his invention, building a total of about 20 pianos. Bartolomeo's final years were filled with disappointment that the piano had not been more fully embraced by others. His invention might have died, too, if some of his pianos had not found their way outside Italy, and if Maffei's description of his innovation had not spread.

Nearly forgotten while still in its infancy, the piano was rediscovered by Gottfried Silbermann, who built on Cristofori's ideas.

Fr. ... Corn. 1
... Viola
Concert

Fr. ... Corn. 2
... Trom. 2

Com. di Caccia

Fr. Ziegler Concert

Fr. Forsch... Concert

Bassono

Directores

Mons. Benda

Fr. Oschatz
Hautbois 2
od. Flaut Traver.

Fr. Kirchhoff
Hautbois 1
Concert

Fr. Landvoigt
Flaut. Traver.
1. Concert

Traverso
Concert

Traverso
Concert

Voigt asfist.

Fr. Lunis

Fr. Funcke
Grand Violon

Gran Violon

Fr. Wenckel
Violoncell.
Concert

Fr. Georius

Cembalo

Fr. Aßbol
Concert

Fr. Gerlach
Concert

Violino Secondo

Fr. Gerlach
Concert

Fr. Hager
Concert

Fr. Auba
Concert

Fr. Probst
Altist

Fr. Schneider

Fr. Schwalbe
Concert

Fr. Ewger
Discantist

Violino Primo

Viola

Fr. ...
Concert

Fr. Wieder

Fr. Roснаgel
Discant.
asfist

Fr. Albrecht

Fr. Crier

NB. Wenn auf dem ...
so spielt Fr. ...
u. Fr. Wiener ...
und wenn Trom ...
so Fr. Aube und
Probst und Fr. ...
Fr. Kirchhoff ...
Travers. Sobald ...
voigt asfist...
gespielet werden

Fr. Gerlach und Fr. ...
auf der Viola ...
Cas B...

Fr. Wieder u. Fr. ...
beyde ... Tenor ...

NB. diese bey dem Sänger
asfistiren... der Viola

Fr. Wieder von der ...
Fr. Schneider von ...
Concert... auf ...

The Germans were credited with inventing the piano for many years until Cristofori's achievement was again widely recognized in the mid-1800s.

German composer Johann Sebastian Bach, who fathered 20 children during his lifetime, was among history's most prolific composers. He wrote religious and secular music, including cantatas, chorales, concertos, and suites.

It was a German named Gottfried Silbermann, best known as an organ builder, who was largely responsible for popularizing Bartolomeo's piano. Historical evidence suggests that Silbermann not only read about but saw one of Bartolomeo's pianos before he set about building his own. Renowned German composer Johann Sebastian Bach tested one of Silbermann's models in 1736. Although intrigued, Bach suggested the instrument needed more work. More than a decade later, Bach played one of Silbermann's pianos before Frederick the Great, delighting the Prussian king, who promptly ordered 15 pianos. Excitement about the piano in Spain, Portugal, Germany, and England ultimately propelled the instrument's rise.

An 18th-century diagram of the piano (opposite); Johann Sebastian Bach playing for Frederick the Great (above).

Before going on to try other instruments, many children today obtain a basic musical understanding on the piano.

Built in 1720, the oldest of three remaining Cristofori pianos is housed at the Metropolitan Museum of Art in New York. The others, built in 1722 and 1726, are at the Instrument Museum in Rome and Leipzig University in Germany, respectively.

Before the time of in-home phonographs and radios, recorded music was played on upright player pianos. Jets of air were pushed through holes on a paper music roll, which caused hammers to strike the strings to sound notes.

By the early 1800s, the forerunners to the piano—the clavichord and harpsichord—had faded from popularity and were no longer produced in great numbers. Instrument makers, meanwhile, continued to refine the piano. They created new shapes—most prominently the upright version so common today. And they added power and range to the relatively delicate sound of Bartolomeo's creation.

Bartolomeo Cristofori's once-neglected invention—his "harpsichord with soft and loud"—finally became an instrument whose presence is commonplace across the world. It is today found on stages, in recording studios, and in living rooms. It is at home in smoky pubs and sunny kindergarten classrooms. And its versatility makes it a part of music in nearly every form. It can provide quiet accompaniment to a soulful singer, or, at the hands of a master pianist, it can fill a great concert hall with sound.

The piano has taken on a variety of physical forms, but the richness and versatility of its sound remain unrivaled.

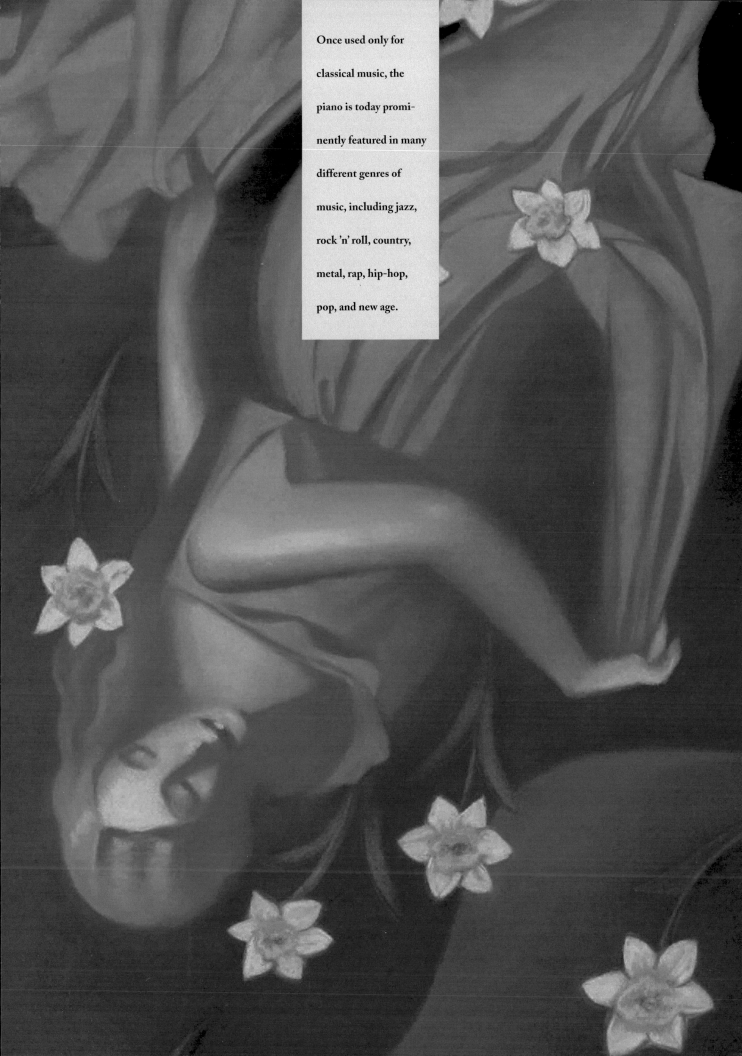

Once used only for
classical music, the
piano is today promi-
nently featured in many
different genres of
music, including jazz,
rock 'n' roll, country,
metal, rap, hip-hop,
pop, and new age.

Wolfgang Amadeus Mozart gained fame as both a composer and a pianist extraordinaire.

The piano also became a most indispensable tool of composers. It has been used famously by musicians ranging from Wolfgang Amadeus Mozart to John Lennon, but its greatest impact may be in the homes and lives of millions of people. To them, the piano is not just a clever machine or beautiful furnishing; it is an instrument that allows just about anyone living just about anywhere to make and enjoy music.

The drawing room was a refined meeting locale that often featured showy displays of furniture and keepsakes.

Well-educated Europeans of the 1720s often gathered in the drawing rooms (large rooms used for entertaining) of wealthy nobles to discuss new music, books, and philosophies.

What in the World?

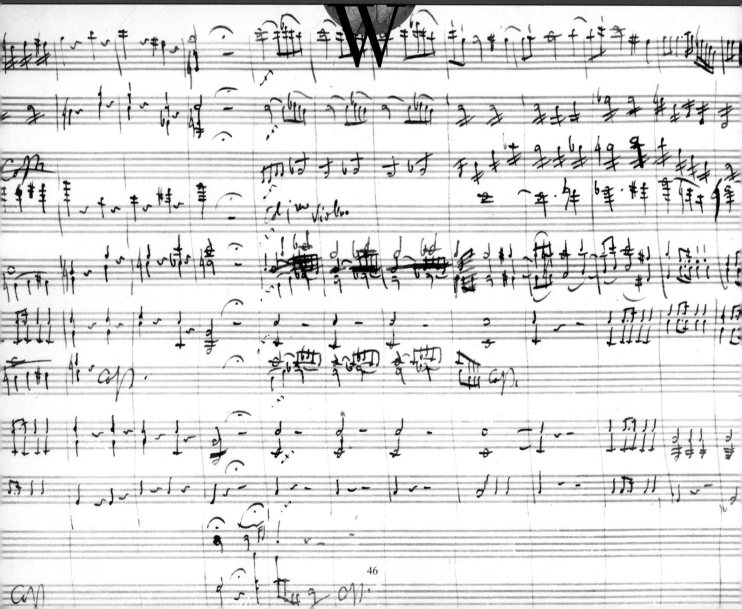

1655   Bartolomeo Cristofori is born in Padua, Italy.

1656   Dutch travelers return from France to describe a "fountain pen" holding its own ink reservoir.

1658   Coffee, billed as a medicine to treat many ailments, is first sold in London.

1670   The Palace of Versailles near Paris is completed, although significant additions begin eight years later.

1681   The first record of an official boxing match in England appears in a newspaper.

1682   English astronomer Edmond Halley studies a comet and accurately predicts when it will again pass Earth.

1685   German composer Johann Sebastian Bach is born in the city of Eisenach.

1689   Cristofori builds his first harpsichord.

1700   Cristofori's invention of the piano is first recorded.

1709   Cristofori publicly reveals his piano and demonstrates it to Roman journalist Scipione Maffei.

1711   Maffei publishes an article describing Cristofori's innovative new keyboard instrument.

1712   Englishman Thomas Newcomen patents the first steam-powered piston engine.

1713   Prince Ferdinando de Medici dies, and Cristofori becomes curator of his instrument collection.

1719   Popular English novelist Daniel Dafoe's *Robinson Crusoe* is published.

1720   The oldest surviving piano is made by Cristofori.

1726   German Gottfried Silbermann constructs a piano based on Cristofori's hammer design.

1729   Benjamin Franklin purchases the *Pennsylvania Gazette,* which becomes the leading newspaper across several American colonies.

1731   Cristofori dies in Florence, Italy.

Copyright

Published by Creative Education
123 South Broad Street, Mankato, Minnesota 56001

Creative Education is an imprint of The Creative Company.
Design by Rita Marshall
Production design by The Design Lab

Photographs by Art Resource, NY (Erich Lessing, The Museum of Modern Art/Licensed by SCALA, The Pierpont Morgan Library, Réunion des Musées Nationaux, Ricco/Maresca Gallery, Scala, Victoria & Albert Museum, London), Corbis (Arte & Immagini srl, Archivo Iconografico, S.A., Bettmann, Michael Boys, Burstein Collection, Christie's Images, Françoise Gervais, Historical Picture Archive, E.O. Hoppé, Hulton–Deutsch Collection, Bob Krist, Leng/Leng, Francis G. Mayer, National Gallery Collection; By kind permission of the Trustees of the National Gallery, London, Gianni Dagli Orti), Getty Images (Lewis W. Hine/George Eastman House, Time Life Pictures)

Illustrations copyright © 1983 Jean-Louis Besson, (37) © 1990 Jean Claverie, (40) © 2006 Etienne Delessert, (27, 48) © 1998 Gary Kelley, (42-43) © 1988 Georges Lemoine, (44) © 1997 Rodica Prato, (19, 35, 41)

Copyright © 2006 Creative Education.
International copyright reserved in all countries. No part of this book may be reproduced in any form without written permission from the publisher.

Library of Congress Cataloging-in-Publication Data
Healy, Nick.
The piano / by Nick Healy.
p. cm. — (What in the world?)
Includes index.
ISBN 1-58341-376-6
1. Piano—Juvenile literature. 2. Cristofori, Bartolomeo, 1655–1731—Juvenile literature. I. Title. II. Series.

ML650.H39 2004   786.2'19—dc22   2004059367

First Edition
9 8 7 6 5 4 3 2 1

Index